Carol Bruggen

Letters to Lucy

about Oliver the Dog

ANDRE DEUTSCH

These letters were written to Lucy
whose short life was filled with love
and happiness

First published in 1986 by
André Deutsch Limited
105 Great Russell Street London WC1B 3LJ

British Library Cataloguing in Publication Data

Bruggen, Carol
    Letters to Lucy.
    I. Title
823'.914[J]   PZ7
ISBN 0-233-97887-9

Dear Lucy,
    We have a new puppy at our house.
His name is Oliver and he's a bad'un.

When he wants a biscuit he sits in his bed,
which is a box by the stove, and looks
positively beautiful and well-behaved.

But the rest of the time he isn't. He eats everything he can reach. The day before yesterday he ate a packet of herbal cigarettes. He didn't like those much, but he persevered.

He even eats Tom's socks, which is strange because everybody else tries to avoid them.

Randolph the cat has a very poor opinion of Oliver and looks down his nose at him. But he is careful to keep his tail out of the way, because Oliver likes to torment it.

He doesn't understand about dogs doing certain things *outside*, so we put newspapers on the kitchen floor. Unfortunately he thinks these are for him to read, so he lifts his leg and pees in between them.

make a piddle

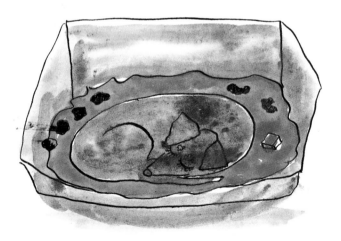

At night he curls up in his bed and goes to sleep so we can all have a bit of peace. But he likes to have a few lumps of coal around him in case he gets hungry and wants a snack.

Give your mummy and daddy and Judith a big hug and kiss from me.

Love and hugs to you
from your friend Carol.

XXXXXXXXXX

(Oliver's footprint)

Dear Lucy,

The other day I noticed that the birds in the tree looked hungry. There was a lot of snow and the worms were staying in bed in their holes instead of coming out to be eaten.

So . . .

I made them a bird-pudding out of bread and milk and margarine and dried fruit and peanuts and old biscuits and they all came down to where the grass usually is (where we sit in the summer) and had breakfast.

However . . .

not long afterwards Tom went out with Oliver to have a good time in the snow and they did until . . .

Oliver noticed the bird-pudding and started to eat it. All the birds cried out in horror and flew back into the tree.

But . . .

when they saw that the funny bird with all those legs was too busy eating the bird-pudding to eat them, they all came down again and finished their breakfast.

(That's Lucy's face peeping through the hole in the wall.)

Randolph has started sitting on top of the booze cupboard, where the hole in the wall by the stairs is, because Oliver can't get hold of his tail when he's up there. But it is nice and warm, and while he's sitting there he falls asleep . . .

and gradually leans further and further and further over. So Oliver sits at the bottom laughing and hoping that he will fall off.

Love to
Mum and Dad
and Judith and
Lucy!
From your friend Carol.
XXXX

Dear Lucy,

Thank you *very* much for your lovely letter and the nice picture of you and Oliver. I have pinned them up on the beam where people can see them but *he* can't eat them. He is getting very big. He thinks that because Randolph can jump high he should be able to as well.

But...

HE CAN'T.

Today I took him for his first walk up the road. He was a bit frightened of the cars but he liked all the different smells and kept lingering at interesting corners. I had hoped that he would do *certain things* that he has been doing on the kitchen floor.

But he didn't.

he sat down and refused to go any further.

So . . .

he drank Randolph's bowl of milk.

Then . . .

He tried to eat the lead.

Then . . .

I had to carry him home. As soon as we entered the house – I won't tell you what he did – but it begins with P. made a big puddle on the floor

Then . . .

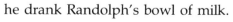

he ate Randolph's bowl of fish.

Then . . .

he ate Randolph's bowl of Munchies.

Then . . .

he ate Randolph's BOWL.
You can tell what a bad 'un he is.

Love to
Mum and Dad and Judith
and to my friend Lucy
from her friend Carol.
XXXX

Love and hugs and a sloppy kiss from Oliver.

Dear Lucy,

I don't know whether you remember when you were quite small we went to see the rabbit who lives across the road. Well, a dog lives there now too. He looks like this from the front

and

like this from the back.

The only way in which you can tell where he's going is if you catch a glimpse of him from the side when he is moving, or (if you can count them) by the tufts; two at the front where his ears are and one at the back round about his tail. His name is Peppy.

Well, Oliver has started to notice things that are not just in *his* kitchen. Last night he heard Peppy barking by the front gate,

and . . .

my word, thought Oliver, that's a fine noise. I wonder if I can do it.

But when he threw back his head and tried to bark all that came out were pretty little bubbles of noise like somebody singing. He looked worried, as well he might.

But he started to practise and ran round and round the kitchen barking at the chairs, the table, the cupboards, and Tom's peanut butter container.

We told him that he had a very good bark and that he could practise again another day

BUT . . .

he was so pleased with himself that he stayed up nearly all night barking in different tones of voice while Peppy went home to bed. This morning he barked at the milkman, at the postman, at the paper boy, and at a man who was going off to work on his bicycle. Then . . .

I went out to do some shopping and he jumped into the second shelf from the top in the vegetable rack and ate a pound of tomatoes.

This . . .

gave him a fat belly and the HICK-UPS.

When he HICKS his ears stay down and when he UPS they stand on end. I daresay later on he will get other things that dogs often get when they have eaten a pound of tomatoes.

Randolph said, if *I* had eaten a pound of tomatoes Murray would have thrown me out of the window into the flower bed but of course, *I'm* not a dog, I'm only an old cat with a blind eye and *nobody* ever pays *any* attention to *me*. But *I* don't mind. *I'll* just *sit* here like the good animal I am until *somebody* thinks of *feeding* me.

Then . . .

when I had put his Munchies in his bowl he sat and listened to Oliver's HICK-UPS and ate his lunch and completely forgot that he was pretending to have a sore eye.

Love to Mum, Dad, Judith and Lucy from your friend Carol and Oliver's hick-ups.
XXXXX

P.S. I think Peppy would send you a big kiss too; if he knew that I was writing to you, and if he could remember which end his ears were at.

Dear Lucy,

Olly has a new five-star dog basket. We noticed that when he was asleep in his box his nose was squashed up and so was his tail end, so that he looked like an accordian. So we thought, we don't want a squashed Olly dog so we had a think.

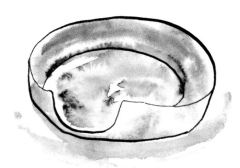

Now Gail, who lives down the road, has a dog called Dylan. He is one of those dogs that go a long way between one end and the other, and he is covered with double chins.

I mean . . .

even his eyes have double chins.

When he was a puppy he used to worry a great deal about his back legs. They always seemed to be so far behind the rest of him.

But . . .

Gail bought him this five-star dog bed and
he discovered that if he led his front legs
into it and settled them down, the others
followed. For a long time he was very
proud and happy, but alas, as time passed
he got BIGGER (he couldn't get any
longer, but he did get much bigger),

until . . .

the day arrived when *none* of him could fit
into the five-star dog bed at all.

Dylan, said Gail, would you like to give
your five-star dog bed to a smaller dog;
say, Oliver. Why not? he replied.

So, instead of being squashed up like
an accordian, now . . .

Olly sleeps in luxury with all his treasures
around him in Dylan's five-star dog bed,

while Dylan sleeps just inside Gail's front
door where he is ready to bite the
postman, burglars and things, and also he
keeps out the draughts.

Now Oliver, as you also know, doesn't approve of cats who give themselves airs, so, with all his usual jolly sense of humour he waits until she is not expecting it, like this (he has a great sense of timing, too,)

I forgot to tell you about Oliver and Josephine. As you know, unlike Randolph, Josephine is a very dignified cat. She goes about with a superior look and sits straight up and down like a town councillor.

then . . .

he barks a loud short sharp bark and Josephine looks as if she had sat on an electric wire.

Ha ha, says Olly joyously.

Much love to Lucy, Mum, Dad and Judith
with hugs and all that from
your friend Carol.
XXXXX

Dear Lucy,

I bought this hat for Oliver. He said, I can't wear *that*. *I'm* a *boy*. *That's* a *girl's* hat. What would my friends in the village say if I went around wearing a *girl's* hat? So I said, shall we send it to Lucy? What a splendid idea, Oliver replied, feeling very relieved, and then . . .

he went outside and disappeared into a snowdrift. Oliver, Oliver, I called, but there was no sign of him. The snow here is very deep and I was a bit anxious in case he came out in Australia.

However . . .

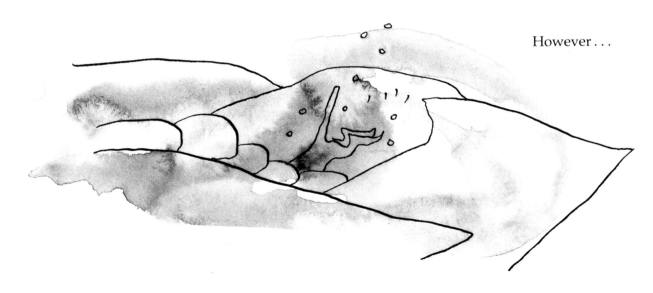

after a long time he emerged from another snowdrift, looking very happy. He asked to be let out again when it was dark and sang a song to the moon.

But . . .

when he came in and ate his supper he was so hungry that he swallowed it all without chewing with his sharp little teeth. And so, a bit later, out came a very ROODE NOYSE. Oliver looked sternly at his tail. Did *you* do that? he said to it accusingly.

Don't tell anybody that I've told you that one.

Love to Mum, Dad, Judith and Lucy
from your friends Carol, Oliver, Randolph
and Josephine with hugs.

XXXX

Dear Lucy,

I forgot to tell you about Murray's bobble cap. One day he left it on the table and you can guess what happened next.

Randolph sat up and said to himself, my word, there's going to be some fun here. And there was. Murray said to Oliver, have you eaten the bobble off my bobble cap? And Oliver could see that there was no point in denying it.

Then . . .

Murray started beating him ALL OVER with what was left of the bobble cap and Oliver thought to himself, I think I'll go for a walk in the garden.

Randolph . . .

began to laugh and the more he laughed
the funnier it seemed so he laughed some
more. He covered his eyes with his paw
and laughed until his belly ached.

Oliver went out into the garden.

Then . . .

Randolph said with tears of happiness streaming down his cheeks. My word, that's done me good. There's not much to laugh at around here nowadays.

Love again, to all of you from all of us, Carol.

XXXX

Dear Lucy,

Many thanks for your beautiful letter. Your writing is very clever. I'm sorry about the chickenpox. I always think it should be called chicken spots, then instead of having to write that difficult word you could just say I have got . . .

Recently we allowed Oliver to explore the house because he doesn't do all that you-know-what inside any more, but asks to go out into the garden.

He liked the bedrooms very much and was missing for a long time. He thought Murray's pillow was a lot more comfortable than even a five-star dog bed.

But . . .

the thing that interested and amused him most on his journey was what he found in the bathroom. Aha, he said, my word, that's a handy object. I always wondered how *they* managed.

Unfortunately . . .

Randolph was asleep in his safe place on top of the refrigerator and unaware of the nasty surprise he was about to have when . . . Oliver, on his way downstairs discovered that he, too, could climb through that hole in the wall.

Lots of love to Judith, Mum and Lucy with this letter delivered not by the postman but by Dad, from your friend Carol.

xxxx

P.S. I forgot to tell you about the giant bone which the butcher sent to Oliver. He was very worried about it because it was the most precious thing he had ever had and he was afraid that some of the *people* might eat it or throw it away,

so . . .

he buried it under the rug and then felt quite happy. Nobody can possibly find it there, he said joyfully.

Love again, Carol.

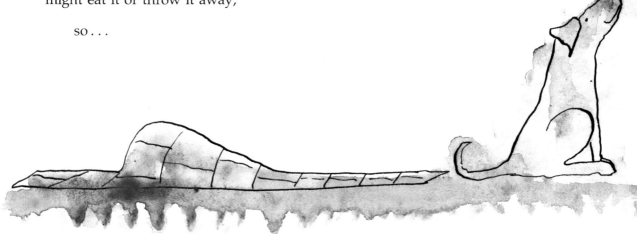

Dear Lucy,

The other day Oliver was sitting in his five-star dog bed chewing something with a thoughtful expression on his face.

Suspecting that it was something he shouldn't have, I made him give it to me. And imagine my surprise to find that it was one of his back teeth. The new tooth had grown up underneath and pushed it out.

Well, Oliver, said I, we have put this under your pillow for the Tooth Fairy to take so you will have to sleep on the chair tonight because there is no pillow in your five-star dog bed.

So . . .

he slept on the chair and the Tooth Fairy came and took his tooth away from under the pillow.

Now then, said the Tooth Fairy, very much perplexed, what am I going to leave him in exchange? If I give him the usual 5p piece he will only eat it, won't he, so that won't do.

So . . .

she flew off to the place where the Tooth Fairies live and struggled all the way back with a huge bone.

Whew, sighed the long suffering Tooth Fairy, I'm glad I don't have to do *that* every night.

But . . .

while Oliver had been asleep, he had dreamed a very happy dream about sheep. He thought he knew where he could find some, so when he went out into the garden, instead of running round and round in circles he went in a straight line up to the back wall and jumped over a place where the stones had fallen down and . . .

Then . . .

a big sheep came across the field and said to Oliver, if you stay on that side of the wall, I'll tell you some jokes and some stories. And Oliver replied, I'd rather chase you up hill and down dale, but if you are not keen on racing I suppose a tale is better than nothing so do tell . . .

the sheep and lambs ran in all directions. My word, thought Oliver, these woollen dogs aren't as friendly as they might be. But at that moment Tom caught him and put him back into the garden and built the wall up so high that he couldn't possibly jump over it again.

But . . .

the sheep's story was very boring, full of baaaaas and when he came back into the house Oliver felt restless and ate a carton of pepper.

This . . .

of course, made him sneeze and he sneezed for a week and five days which gave the sheep time to get back up the hill to his friends.

Love to Lucy and Judith and Mum and Dad
from their friend Carol and Old Sneezy.
XXXX

Dear Lucy

This was the week that all the boy scouts did jobs for people. A friend of ours, Crispin, who is a boy scout, came and cleared the front yard. He puffed and panted and got a bit red in the face, but he made such a good job of it that I gave him £1.

My word, thought Oliver, I think I'd like to be a dog scout. But he couldn't decide what to do, until he went into the garden and saw the clothes on the washing line blowing in the wind. They seemed to him to be struggling.

The poor things, thought Oliver, they want to get down and they can't. I'll do my good-deed-job.

So . . .

he jumped up and caught hold of Tom's shirt. My word, thought Oliver, I'm going to enjoy being a dog scout, and he swung joyfully to and fro.

Then . . .

the pegs started to leap off the clothes' line and he knew that he was really being very helpful indeed.

So . . .

he puffed and he panted and persevered until he had set all the clothes free, then he carried them away to different parts of the garden.

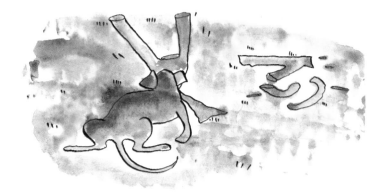

My word . . .

thought Oliver, quietly eating Tom's shirt in the daffodils, they're going to be awfully pleased with me.

And . . .

he might almost have been right because when he went back into the house he found that Tom had kindly left all his pocket money on the edge of the table.

It's uncommonly good of the old chap to pay me so much money for my good-deed-job, thought Oliver.

And . . .

he found that it was delicious.

He ate one whole pound note, one half pound note and he just chewed the third one into little pieces. One mustn't be greedy, he said aloud.

Then . . .

feeling very glad to be a good-dog-scout he curled up in his five-star dog bed for a nap.

Possibly I ate too quickly, he thought with a yawn, I think I feel HICK-UPS coming on.

I hope to see you all very soon.

In the meantime, love to Mum and Dad and Judith and Lucy and . . . from your friend who thinks about you a lot, Carol.

XXXX

Dear Lucy,

    We were all very excited to hear that you have got Judith AND a baby brother now. Your mum says that you are a great help to her, looking after him. Which is more than I can say of SOME, for instance your friend and mine who found the empty dog meat tin.

    Uh-huh, said Oliver, just a trifle left in this, down at the bottom, I feel.

    So . . .

    he found a nice quiet corner and settled down to investigate.

    Not very easy to get, said Oliver thoughtfully, pushing his whole nose into the tin.

    Needless to say . . .

he overdid it, as usual. He ran around the house bumping into things.

    Now I know what an elephant feels like, he thought. But this is ridiculous. I shall be laughed at by all the other dogs. They will think I have been playing K-9.

    Fortunately . . .

when he took hold of it with both his spare front paws it began to loosen. All at once it popped off and out came his nose, rather pink and puffy but just his own usual nose still.

My word, thought Oliver, that was close.

Now it is funny how often one's plans coincide with somebody else's plans. Just at that moment I was in the bathroom running the bathwater.

My word . . .

thought Oliver, what a lot of drinking water. I'm sure that would cool down a fellow's hot nose.

So . . .

he leaned over as far as he could and cooled his nose.

The water was hot, which surprised him, and he leaned a bit further to see whether the water on the other side of the drinking tub was hot too.

To cut a long story short . . . .

. . .Pass the soap, dear.
I'm feeling a trifle hungry

This is LOVELY, said Oliver. Pass the soap, dear (he always calls me dear when he wants something) . . .

Lots of love to Judith, John, Mum, Dad and Lucy from your friend Carol.

Dear Lucy,

Once upon a time, so long ago that it was before you were even born, we had a dog called Rags. It was a good name for him because he *was* very raggy. Sometimes he came home covered with what can only be called cow-plop, and often little things would hop out of his fur and enjoy themselves on people's trouser legs.

He was already a grown-up dog when he came to live with us because we got him from the place where you find dogs that people have lost.

He looked after Josephine the cat when she was a kitten, long before she married Winston and Randolph was born, and as she grew up he had happy times showing her around the countryside because, unlike Oliver, he was a dog who could always find the right thing to say to a cat.

Now one day when we had had him for a long time, many years, and he and Josephine were very good friends, he happened to die one day,

So . . .

he went to heaven where there are always seagulls to chase and waves to bark at and interesting things to do. And when you fall down and scrape your leg it doesn't hurt, and all that sort of thing, you know.

Well, now Josephine has died too, so she is being shown around the countryside in heaven by Rags, going for walks by lovely streams and helping him to do his rounds checking up on dog pee messages on the trees,

then . . .

curling up with him all warm and cosy at night under the stars.

Well, as you know, Josephine, though she was a dear and lovable cat, got a bit bad-tempered with Randolph in her old age. So now that she isn't here to tell him off any more, he is suddenly very brave and courageous – as you will realize when I tell you that Oliver found him . . .

asleep in the five-star dog bed.

Ahem, excuse me, old fellow, excuse *me*, I'm sorry to *disturb* you, but do you realize where you *are*. I mean, where you actually are sleeping at this very moment in time? I mean, you are asleep in MY BEST FIVE-STAR dog basket. Not just any old basket, or even any old DOG basket, but MY FIVE-STAR ONE.

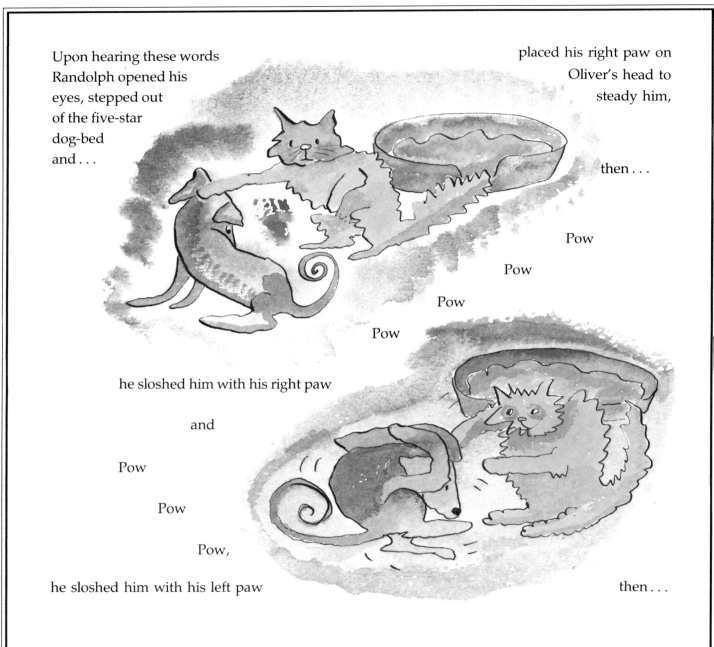

Upon hearing these words Randolph opened his eyes, stepped out of the five-star dog-bed and . . .

placed his right paw on Oliver's head to steady him,

then . . .

Pow

Pow

Pow

Pow

he sloshed him with his right paw

and

Pow

Pow

Pow,

he sloshed him with his left paw

then . . .

he climbed back into the five-star dog bed
and went to sleep again.

Ah, thought Oliver wisely, I said
something to offend him.

So . . .

he woke Randolph up very gently and
said, I say, old chap, I didn't mean to
upset you, I just meant, look, I mean,
would you be kind enough to *move over?*

*Love to Lucy
and Judith and John and Mum and Dad
from your always friend Carol*

XXXX

Dear Lucy,

It was very nice to see you all at home the other day looking so fit and well and you've grown huge and so has Judith and John's got started already. I hope I shall either come again to see you soon or you will all come here. The next time I come to your house I'd like to go underneath all the leaves on that willow tree outside at the front. I bet that's a lovely place to hide.

Now this picture up here shows Oliver passing the time of day by chewing up my sweeping brush. Not doing anybody any harm, you understand, just minding his own business.

Imagine, therefore, his horror to see . . .

looking through his going-in and coming-out window, A FACE. Not only was there a face, but a hand with a big cloth in it wiping round and round the glass.

Oliver was FURIOUS.

Then a ladder went up outside the window, and FEET dangled about in front of his nose.

   The *cheek* of it, said Oliver indignantly, the absolute *cheek* of it.

   And . . .

he barked and he barked and he BARKED.

   I must warn my people of this great danger to the household, thought Oliver, conscious of great responsibility, so he barked even louder and . . .

the window-cleaner smiled at him through the upstairs window.

   My goodness gracious me and my word, this is terrible, thought Oliver,

and he tried baring his fangs at the intruder and growling ferociously.

But . . .

nobody paid any attention to him at all.

Uh-huh, thought Oliver. A real tough cookie, this guy. He went into the bedroom and climbed up on to a chair in order to be a bit taller.

But the more he barked the more the window-cleaner smiled and this INFURIATED Oliver.

He followed the window-cleaner from one room to another until they came to one in which the window was OPEN.

Then . . .

the window-cleaner leaned inside and waved at Oliver before he closed it to get on with his work.

The liberty. The diabolical liberty, thought Oliver. No burglar takes liberties with my people's house and gets away with it. I'll have his trouser leg for that.

And . . .

when the window-cleaner came to the door to be paid, he did.

OLIVER, we all said, WHAT have you done? This is our friend Colin, the window-cleaner, not a burglar.

Uh-huh, said Oliver in a small voice, I think . . .

I have committed a boo-boo.
And . . .

he looked so sad and crestfallen that Colin said, never mind, he was doing his best.

And . . .

he patted Oliver on the head.

I *was* doing my best, wasn't I, said Oliver gratefully and, he thought to himself, nobody can do better than that, even if there's no burglar.

Love to you all,
Mum, Dad, Judith, Lucy, John
and all those beans in the garden,
from your friend Carol